Canada Goose at Cattail Lane

SMITHSONIAN'S BACKYARD

For Stephanie, the precious last gosling in our parade—J.H.

To Stanley Stegos, whose wisdom and knowledge have helped me throughout my career and throughout my life—D.S.

Published by Soundprints, an imprint of Trudy Corporation, Norwalk, Connecticut.

Book design: Shields & Partners, Westport, CT
Editor: Laura Gates Galvin
Book layout: Marcin D. Pilchowski

First Edition 2005
10 9 8 7 6 5 4 3
Printed in Indonesia

Acknowledgments:
Our very special thanks to Dr. Gary R. Graves of the Division of Vertebrate Zoology at the Smithsonian Institution's National Museum of Natural History for his curatorial review.
Soundprints would like to thank Ellen Nanney and Katie Mann at the Smithsonian Institution's Office of Product Development and Licensing for their help in the creation of this book.

Library of Congress Cataloging-in-Publication Data is on file with the publisher and the Library of Congress.

Canada Goose at Cattail Lane

by Janet Halfmann
Illustrated by Daniel J. Stegos

Soundprints®
Where Children Discover...

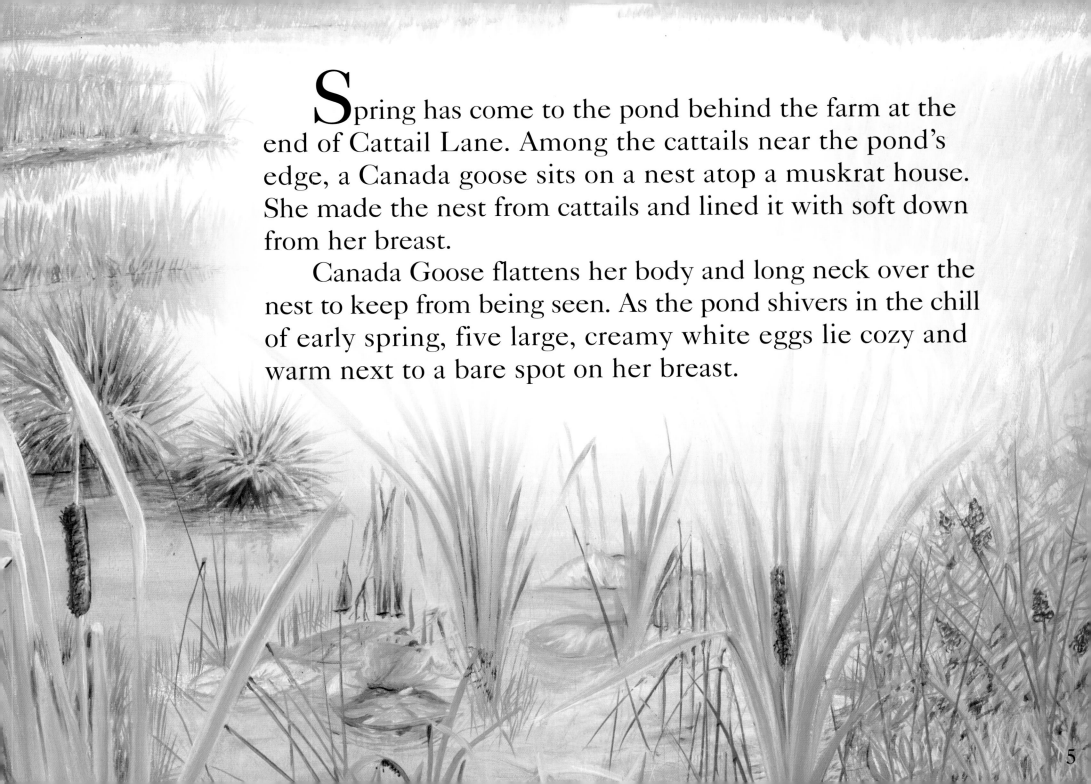

Spring has come to the pond behind the farm at the end of Cattail Lane. Among the cattails near the pond's edge, a Canada goose sits on a nest atop a muskrat house. She made the nest from cattails and lined it with soft down from her breast.

Canada Goose flattens her body and long neck over the nest to keep from being seen. As the pond shivers in the chill of early spring, five large, creamy white eggs lie cozy and warm next to a bare spot on her breast.

Canada Goose was born on this pond three years ago. Now she has returned to have her first babies. Her mate—a gander—swims nearby to guard her and the eggs. The two are mates for life.

One day, another Canada goose swims close to the nest. The gander lowers his head and hisses angrily. He charges at the unwelcome visitor, and the other goose swims away.

7

Night and day, Canada Goose sits on the nest. For a short time every morning and afternoon, she leaves to eat and take a bath. Before she goes, she pulls a cover of gray down over the eggs to keep them warm and hidden.

To stay close to the nest, she feeds on duckweed floating in the pond. The gander accompanies her to keep her safe.

After her snack, Canada Goose stands over the nest. She plucks more down from her breast and lets water from her feathers drip onto the eggs to keep them moist. She settles on the nest, pushing back the down cover with her feet. She turns the eggs over so they will warm evenly, something she does often.

Nearly one month has passed. As Canada Goose sits on her nest, she hears peeping coming from inside the eggs. The unborn babies are telling one another that it is time to hatch. The gander moves in closer to guard the family.

Peck, *peck*, *peck*. One after another, the babies peck a hole in their shells. They hammer away for more than a day to break free. The newly hatched babies are covered with down and their eyes are open. They are wet and very tired from the hard work of hatching.

For the first day and night, Canada Goose keeps them tucked under her in the warm nest. While they sleep, their thick down dries to a fluffy yellow.

15

Early the next morning, the goslings are ready to see the world. Canada Goose leads them to the water's edge. She enters first and calls *kum*, *kum*, *kum*. One after the other, the goslings plop in. With their fluffy down, they float like little corks.

As Canada Goose leads, the little ones paddle behind her with their webbed feet. The gander falls in line at the end of the gosling parade.

After a nap on shore under Canada Goose's wing, the goslings are led to a green spot that has short, new grass. They soon learn to nip off grass with their bills, just like their parents do.

One gosling wanders into the tall grass. Which way is out? *Eep-peep-peep* calls the lost gosling. Canada Goose guides the little one back to the family. The gosling now calls happily, *wheeoo, wheeoo, wheeoo.*

A few days later, as the family swims on the pond, a gull watches from high in the air. Suddenly, the gull dives toward the goslings. But Canada Goose isn't concerned. She knows that the goslings can handle this attack on their own.

And she's right. In a flash, the goslings scatter in all directions. The one nearest the gull disappears under the water. The gull dives at another gosling, but she also escapes. The gull flies away to look for an easier meal.

As the goslings grow, their yellow down fades to gray. Now, Canada Goose and the gander teach them to dip for food in the pond. Bottoms up! The goslings stick their heads into the water and tip their tails straight up. They grab pondweed and other plants with their bills.

The tiniest gosling keeps popping back up. He is still too fluffy to dip well. But he keeps trying, and in a few days he, too, is filling his tummy with pondweed.

Splish, *splash*, it's time for a bath! Canada Goose and her goslings flap their wings in the water and flip over to wash their backs. Once clean, they preen. Using their bills, they take oil from a place near the tail. They rub the oil into their feathers to make the feathers waterproof.

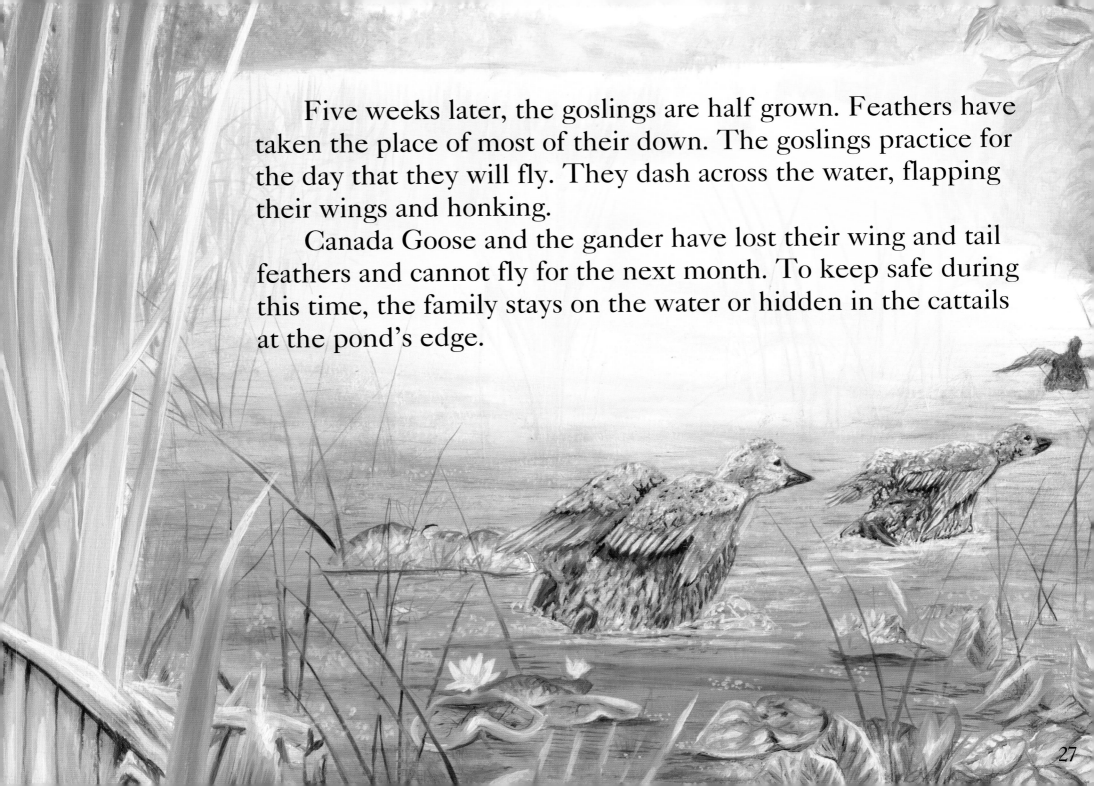

Five weeks later, the goslings are half grown. Feathers have taken the place of most of their down. The goslings practice for the day that they will fly. They dash across the water, flapping their wings and honking.

Canada Goose and the gander have lost their wing and tail feathers and cannot fly for the next month. To keep safe during this time, the family stays on the water or hidden in the cattails at the pond's edge.

By late summer, Canada Goose and the gander have grown new flight feathers. As they try out their new feathers, the young geese take their first flights. Before long, the young are flying from one end of the pond to the other, and then flying over neighboring ponds as well.

Early one August morning, the gander honks that it is time to go. Canada Goose lifts off to lead the way and the young follow. The gander guards the rear. Canada Goose leads the family away from the pond to join other goose families at a better feeding spot miles away.

But come next spring, Canada Goose and her mate will return to the pond once again to raise another family of goslings among the cattails.

About the Canada Goose

The Canada goose is the most abundant and widespread wild goose in North America. It occurs throughout the United States and Canada and also in northern Mexico. There are eleven subspecies, or types, of Canada geese, ranging in size from 3 to 12 pounds. The smallest types cackle and the largest ones honk.

The goose featured in this story is the largest of the group, the giant Canada goose. These geese nest in spring and summer in many parts of the United States and southern Canada. Giant Canada geese tend to spend the winter in the same area where they nest or only travel short distances. Such geese are sometimes called resident geese.

The number of giant Canada geese and other resident geese has exploded in recent years. Sometimes large flocks gather in city parks, on golf courses, or in farm fields and are considered pests.

Many other Canada geese migrate or travel long distances between their nesting and wintering grounds. The majority of these geese nest in northern Canada and Alaska and fly south for the winter in the continental United States. As the geese travel—sometimes more than a thousand miles—they fly in honking V-shapes high in the sky.

All Canada geese are dedicated parents. The female sits on the nest and the male guards her. The male is very protective and will attack intruders, including people, by striking them with his wings or nipping them with his beak. Young geese remain with their parents through the first year and the family travels together. Canada geese can live a long time—ten years or more.

Glossary

cattails: Tall plants that grow in shallow water and have long, furry brown flower spikes.

down: Fine, soft feathers of birds.

duckweed: Tiny, floating pond plants with hanging roots.

gander: A male goose; female is called goose.

goslings: Young geese.

muskrat: Brown water animal that looks like a large rat.

muskrat house: High mound nest that the muskrat builds with cattails in the water.

pondweed: A kind of plant that is rooted in the mud of a pond.

preen: To use the bill to clean, straighten, and waterproof feathers.

webbed feet: Feet with pieces of skin joining the toes to help with swimming.

Points of Interest in this Book

pp. 4-5: muskrat.
pp. 12-13: dragonfly.
pp. 16-17: turtle.

pp. 28-29: water lily flower, large-mouth bass. The artist has depicted his grandfather, Stanley Stegos, in the boat.